STAN LEE PRESENTS

GW01191241

The DEATH of CAPTAIN MARVEL

By
JIM STARLIN

COLORED BY: **STEVE OLIFF**
LETTERED BY: **JAMES NOVAK**
EDITED BY: **AL MILGROM**
EDITOR-IN-CHIEF: **JIM SHOOTER**

7th PRINTING
ISBN# 0-939766-11-6

In introduction, little need be said of Captain Marvel. His life has been spent playing the role of warrior. When he realized the limitations inherent in such a life he showed the greatest courage in his warrior's heart, the courage to change, and he sought a path of peace. It was a path circumstances seldom allowed him to follow, but the desire was there. Let us hope that where his path now leads him, he will at last *find* peace.

I thank Jim Starlin (perhaps the man most closely associated with our Kree Captain) for his extraordinary portrayal of Mar-vell's adventures, including this , his last.

Allen Milgrom
2/3/82

THE DEATH OF CAPTAIN MARVEL
I WAS BORN MAR-VELL, A SON OF THE KREE EMPIRE.
ON EARTH, MY NAME FELL VICTIM TO AN ALIEN TONGUE AND I BECAME KNOWN AS MARVEL ...CAPTAIN MARVEL.
THE FOLLOWING IS A JOURNAL OF MY LIFE SINCE I LEFT KREE-LAR; MY ADVENTURES, MY VICTORIES, MY MISTAKES.
MY HOPE IN RECORDING THIS MINI-AUTOBIOGRAPHY IS THAT IT MAY PROVE OF SOME USE TO THOSE I LEAVE BEHIND.

IT ALL BEGAN ON A KREE SCOUT SHIP WHICH MADE AN UNDETECTED LANDING BACK ON EARTH IN *1967*.

THE EXPEDITION WAS ON A SECRET *SPY MISSION*. ITS ASSIGNMENT WAS TO STUDY THE PLANET'S DEFENSES AND POPULACE.

EARTH WAS ON THE DESPOTIC KREE EMPIRE'S LIST OF FUTURE *PLANETARY CONQUESTS*.

I WAS PART OF THAT SCOUT SHIP'S CREW.

I WAS A *KREE WARRIOR*, A CAPTAIN. I WAS SLATED TO BE THE MISSION'S CHIEF *FIELD AGENT*.

ALSO AMONG THE SHIP'S COMPLEMENT WAS ONE COMMUNICATIONS OFFICER *UNA*. I LOVED THIS WOMAN.

BUT MY LOVE WAS DOOMED. FOR THE SHIP'S COMMANDER WAS A COLONEL *YON-ROGG* WHOSE HATRED FOR ME AND LUST FOR UNA WOULD PROVE OUR DOWNFALL.

SO I BEGAN MY MISSION... I BEGAN TO STUDY THE PEOPLE OF EARTH.

BUT THE MORE I LEARNED OF THIS TARGET PLANET, THE MORE *REPULSED* I BECAME AT THE THOUGHT OF THE TYRANNICAL KREE *BESPOILING* THIS LOVELY WORLD AND *ENSLAVING* ITS HAPLESS POPULATION.

I SHARED THESE THOUGHTS WITH *UNA* WHO EVENTUALLY CAME OVER TO MY POINT OF VIEW.

UNFORTUNATELY *YON-ROGG* FOUND US OUT AND TOOK MEASURES TO ASSURE MY *DEATH* SO THAT HE WOULD HAVE A CLEAR FIELD FOR UNA'S AFFECTIONS.

HE SET A TRAP FOR ME ...ARRANGED IT SO I FELL INTO THE HANDS OF THE KREE'S ANCIENT ENEMIES, THE *AAKON.*

I ESCAPED, BUT *UNA* ACCIDENTLY FELL VICTIM TO YON-ROGG'S TREACHERY.

HEARTBROKEN, I *DESERTED* THE KREE. THE *EARTHLINGS* WERE FAR FROM PERFECT BUT WITHIN THEIR COLLECTIVE SOUL I SENSED THE *POTENTIAL FOR GREATNESS.*

I SWORE THEN I WOULD *DEFEND* THEM AGAINST MY HOMEWORLD'S *DARK APPETITE.*

SO THE OLD CAPT. MAR-VELL DIED AND THE *NEW CAPTAIN MARVEL* WAS BORN.

I BECAME EARTH'S *COSMIC PROTECTOR* AND EVENTUALLY AIDED MY NEW HOMEWORLD IN RIDDING ITSELF OF THE THREAT OF THE EVIL KREE EMPIRE.

BUT THE KREE WERE NOT THE ONLY STELLAR RACE THAT COVETED EARTH'S *NATURAL RICHES.* TIME AND AGAIN I WAS CALLED UPON TO SAVE MY ADOPTED HOME.

I WAS GREATLY AIDED IN THIS TASK...

...BY A BEING NAMED *EON* WHO GRANTED ME THE POWER OF *COSMIC AWARENESS.*

SO THE YEARS PASSED AND WITH THEM PASSED WHAT SEEMED LIKE AN ENDLESS LINE OF *VILLAINS* AND WOULD-BE *CONQUERERS.*

I BEGAN TO TIRE.

FORTUNATELY, IN RECENT YEARS, OTHERS OF *GREAT POWER* HAVE COME ALONG TO RELIEVE ME IN THIS ETERNAL BATTLE OF *GOOD* VERSUS *EVIL.*

OF LATE, I'VE BEEN ENJOYING A STATE OF SEMI-RETIREMENT ON *TITAN,* A SATELLITE OF *SATURN.*

TITAN IS A WONDROUS PLACE. ITS OUTER HUSK IS A BARREN, AMMONIA ENSHROUDED DESERT, BUT BENEATH ITS SURFACE LIES A *FUTURISTIC PARADISE*.

THIS WORLD IS JUSTLY RULED BY A DEMI-GOD NAMED *MENTOR* AND HIS SON, *EROS*. I MET THEM YEARS AGO WHEN...

...I HAD TO BATTLE MENTOR'S OTHER SON, THE EVIL *THANOS*.

HE EASILY PROVED HIMSELF THE MOST *DANGEROUS FOE* I EVER FACED.

IN FACT, THANOS IS THE REASON FOR THIS VOYAGE.

DURING OUR LAST CONFLICT THANOS WAS *KILLED*... TURNED TO *STONE*.

HE HAD SOUGHT TO DESTROY OUR ENTIRE SOLAR SYSTEM AS A *SACRIFICE* TO *DEATH*. HIS END WAS GRIM BUT FITTING...

MAR-VELL, WE'RE ALMOST THERE!

SAY, WHAT ARE YOU UP TO BACK HERE?

JUST DOING A LITTLE RECORDING.

I'M PREPARING AN *AUDIO FILE* OF MY LIFE AND ...'ADVENTURES' FOR THE *AVENGERS* AND OTHER EARTH SUPER HEROES.

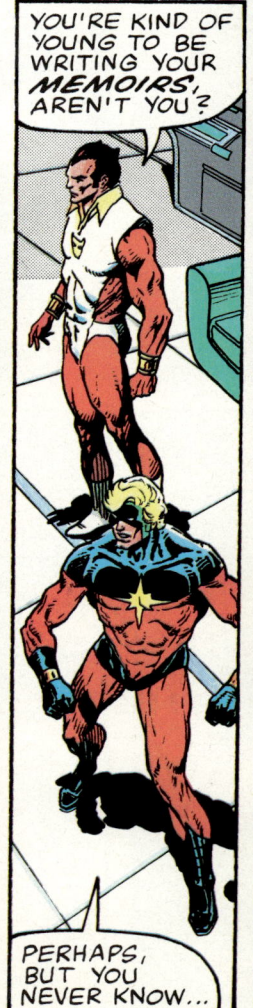

YOU'RE KIND OF YOUNG TO BE WRITING YOUR *MEMOIRS*, AREN'T YOU?

PERHAPS, BUT YOU NEVER KNOW...

"I WAS WITH THE **AVENGERS** WHEN THEY TOWED THANOS'S ARK OUT HERE PAST PLUTO AND ABANDONED IT.

THEY FIGURED IT WASN'T LIKELY TO FALL INTO THE **WRONG HANDS** THIS FAR OUT.

"THANOS RAN HIS ENTIRE OPERATION FROM HERE. THIS WAS HIS **SPACE FLEET'S** CONTROL CENTER. IT WAS ON THIS SHIP HE CREATED THE WEAPON THAT WAS MEANT TO **DESTROY OUR SUN.**

"HE ALSO DIED HERE.

"IT TOOK THE COMBINED POWER OF THE **AVENGERS**, THE **THING, ADAM WARLOCK, SPIDER-MAN** AND MYSELF TO THWART THANOS'S MAD PLANS.

"IT WAS **ADAM WARLOCK** WHO FINALLY STRUCK THANOS DOWN."

HE REACHED OUT FROM HIS **OWN GRAVE** AND SAVED OUR SOLAR SYSTEM.

IT ALL HAPPENED HERE IN THESE DARKENED HALLS. THE **BLACKNESS** OF **OBLIVION** NEARLY CLAIMED US ALL.

BUT, AT THE LAST MOMENT, A **GOLDEN WARRIOR** SAVED US. SO THE **LIGHT** YET SHINES AND **LIFE** CONTINUES.

BUT ALL CONFLICT HAS ITS PRICE. THIS TIME IT COST THE UNIVERSE THE LIFE OF ONE OF ITS HEROES, **ADAM WARLOCK.**

IT COST YOU A *SON.*

HE WAS BORN A *DEMI-GOD.*

HE WAS *POWER* ALMOST WITHOUT END.

HE GAVE HIS HEART TO DEATH.

HE DIED ATTEMPTING TO SATISFY THAT DARK, *UNREQUITED LOVE.*

HE WAS *THANOS* OF *TITAN.*

HE DIED ENCASED IN *STONE* AS HARD AS HIS OWN *HEART.*

BY THE GREAT SPIRIT! I HAD NO IDEA IT WAS LIKE THIS...

THANK YOU, FATHER, FOR ALLOWING US TO TAKE MY BROTHER'S BODY FROM THIS PLACE.

THANOS WAS A VILLAIN... HIS CRIMES HAVE BESMIRCHED THE *HONOR* OF TITAN *FOREVER*... HIS FATE WAS *JUST*...

...BUT HE WAS MY *SON* AND I CANNOT ALLOW HIM TO SPEND ETERNITY ENTOMBED HERE... NO MATTER *WHAT* HE DID.

WE WILL RETURN HIS BODY TO TITAN AND THE *ROYAL CRYPT*.

THIS *PLATFORM*... WASN'T HERE LAST TIME *I* WAS HERE...

...IT ALMOST LOOKS LIKE AN ALTAR.

THERE'S SOMETHING *WRONG* HERE.

SUDDENLY, MAR-VELL'S EVERY SENSE BLAZES TO RAZOR SHARP ALERTNESS...

HIS SPHERE OF BEING EXPANDS...

ALL THAT IS ABOUT HIM IS GRASPED AND RECOGNIZED...

FOR NOTHING CAN ESCAPE HIS *COSMIC AWARENESS*...

MENTOR! EROS! BEWARE!

DIE, INFIDELS!

WHAT THE--?

SUDDENLY THE TRIO IS SURROUNDED.

BUT SUR-ROUNDING CITIZENS OF TITAN IS ONE THING...

...KILLING SUCH MEN IS ANOTHER MATTER.

FOR TITANS DEAL IN POWER.

THE BATTLE RAGES ON, FATHER AND SON MOW DOWN THEIR ATTACKERS WITH DEVASTATING PRE-CISION. THEN, THE UNEXPEC-TED HAP-PENS.

TWO RAIDERS IN JET PACKS SOAR INTO THE HALL. IT'S OBVIOUS THAT THE TWO TITANS ARE TOO PREOCCUPIED WITH MATTERS AT GROUND LEVEL TO DEFEND THEMSELVES FROM THE IMMINENT AIRBORNE ASSAULT.

BY HALA! I HAD HOPED TO SIT THIS FIGHT OUT, BUT I GUESS THE FATES JUST AREN'T GOING TO ALLOW IT!

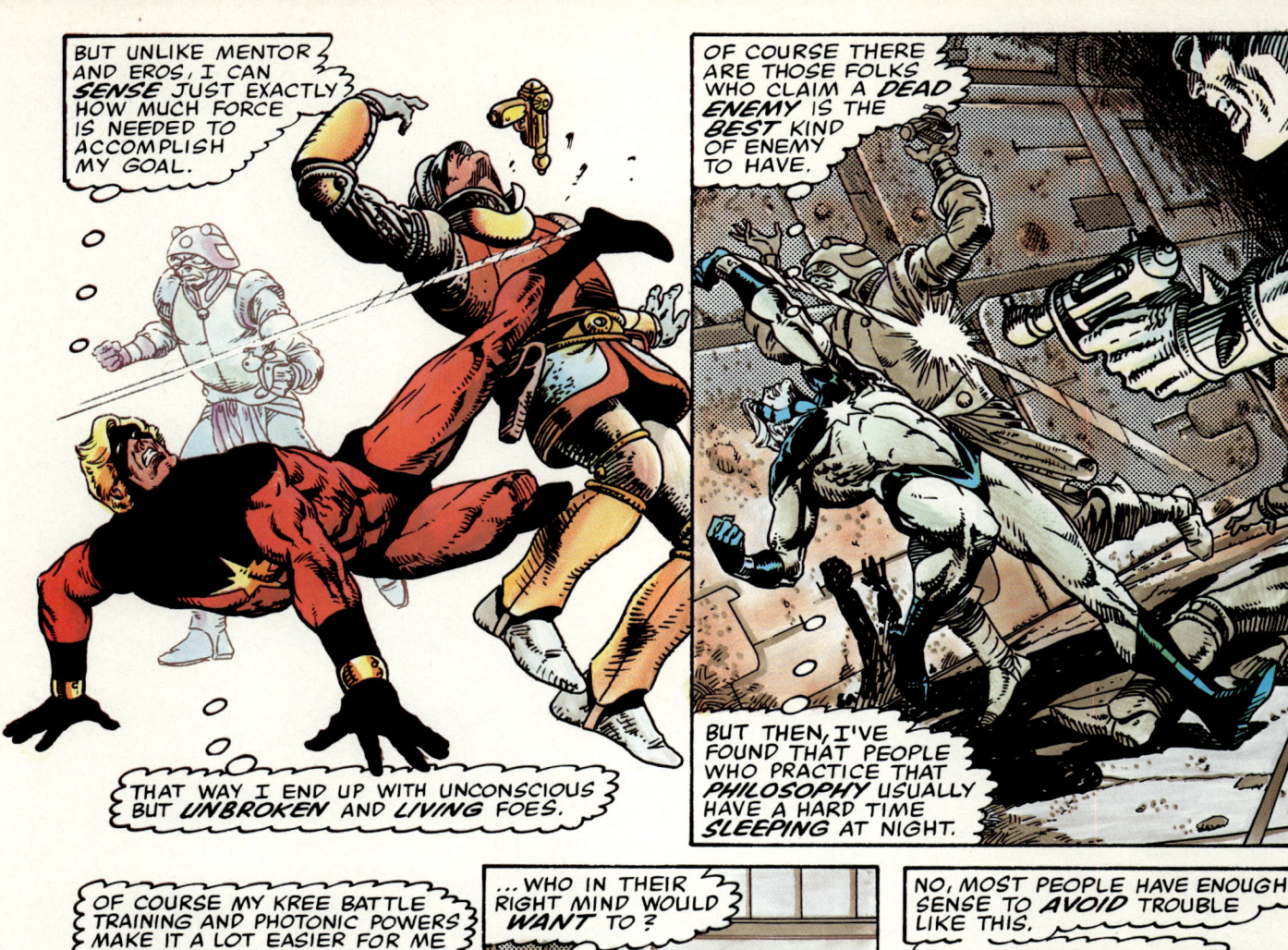

BUT UNLIKE MENTOR AND EROS, I CAN *SENSE* JUST EXACTLY HOW MUCH FORCE IS NEEDED TO ACCOMPLISH MY GOAL.

THAT WAY I END UP WITH UNCONSCIOUS BUT *UNBROKEN* AND *LIVING* FOES.

OF COURSE THERE ARE THOSE FOLKS WHO CLAIM A *DEAD ENEMY* IS THE *BEST* KIND OF ENEMY TO HAVE.

BUT THEN, I'VE FOUND THAT PEOPLE WHO PRACTICE THAT *PHILOSOPHY* USUALLY HAVE A HARD TIME *SLEEPING* AT NIGHT.

OF COURSE MY KREE BATTLE TRAINING AND PHOTONIC POWERS MAKE IT A LOT EASIER FOR ME THAN FOR MOST FOLKS.

THERE AREN'T MANY AROUND WHO CAN *DODGE* A LASER SHOT FIRED AT *POINT BLANK* RANGE LIKE THIS.

BUT FOR THAT MATTER...

...WHO IN THEIR RIGHT MIND WOULD *WANT* TO?

NO, MOST PEOPLE HAVE ENOUGH SENSE TO *AVOID* TROUBLE LIKE THIS.

I'VE BEEN TRYING TO FOLLOW THEIR EXAMPLE, BUT SOMETIMES IT'S JUST NOT EASY TO *SIDESTEP* TROUBLE.

SOMETIMES, BUT NOT ALWAYS.

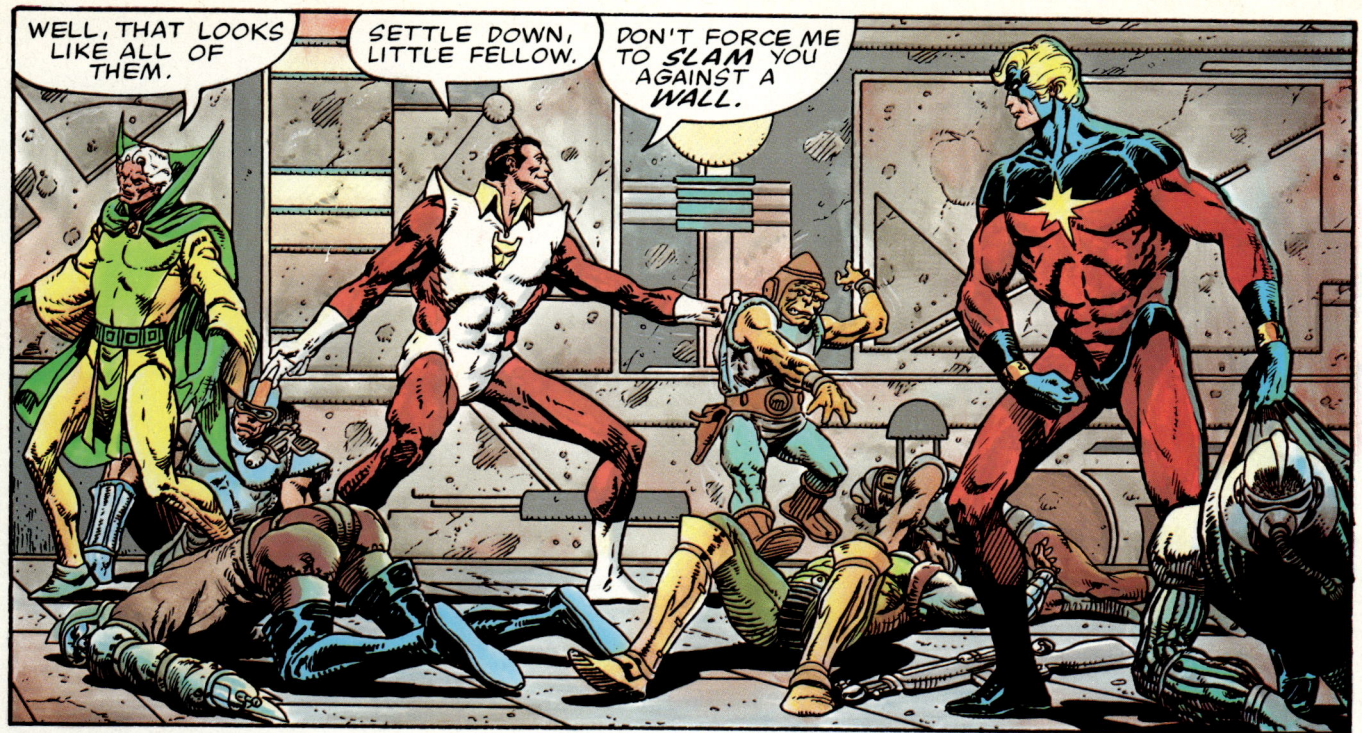

WELL, THAT LOOKS LIKE ALL OF THEM.

SETTLE DOWN, LITTLE FELLOW.

DON'T FORCE ME TO *SLAM* YOU AGAINST A *WALL.*

'*WHEW'*... I'M AFRAID THE EASY LIFE IS CATCHING UP WITH ME.

THIS SORT OF *MELEE* IS GETTING TO BE *TOO MUCH* FOR ME.

WELL, YOU CAN RELAX IF YOU LIKE...

...BUT I WANT TO FIND OUT WHAT THIS *AMBUSH* WAS ALL ABOUT.

I THINK I SEE SOMEONE STILL *CON-SCIOUS* WHO'S *BIG* ENOUGH FOR ME TO GET THAT INFORMA-TION OUT OF.

YOU! WHY DID YOU ATTACK US?

WHO ARE YOU?

WE ARE THE CHILDREN OF *THANOS.*

HE LEAD US ON A QUEST FOR GLORY, WE FOUGHT AND DIED BY HIS SIDE.

HIS DREAMS ARE *OURS.*

BUT HIS DREAMS ARE AS *DEAD* AS HE.

NO! HE BUT RESTS. HE PROMISED US A NEW LIFE AND WOULD NOT LET DOWN THOSE WHO HONOR HIS NAME.

FOR HE IS THE *MASTER* AND IS *OMNIPOTENT.* HE SHALL RETURN AND THE DAY OF *BLOOD* AND *GLORY* WILL AT LAST BE UPON US.

SO WE AWAIT HIS *RESURRECTION.*

BY HALA! THEY WORSHIP *THANOS* AS A GOD...

...AND ARE *WAITING* FOR HIM TO COME BACK FROM THE *DEAD!*

YOU, FOOLS!! CAN YOU TRULY BE SO *BLIND?!*

DO YOU REALLY NOT SEE MY SON FOR WHAT HE WAS *?!*

HE WAS AN *EVIL LUNATIC* WHO *USED* YOU AND WOULD HAVE *SACRIFICED* YOU WITHOUT A SECOND THOUGHT OR REMORSE!

HIS PROMISE OF A *NEW LIFE* WOULD HAVE PROVEN TO BE *DEATH* AND *OBLIVION.*

BUT YOU *MORONS* REPAY HIS TREACHERY WITH BLIND *WOR-SHIP!*

YOU AWAIT HIS RESURRECTION WITH PRAYERS ON YOUR LIPS... *UNBE-LIEVABLE!!*

WELL, WAIT NO MORE!

FOR I'VE COME TO TAKE HIS BODY *HOME,* AND PLAN TO DESTROY THIS *ARK,* THIS LAST TESTAMENT OF HIS INSANE VILLAINY.

SO, GO... LEAVE THIS PLACE OF EVIL AND BEGIN THAT *NEW LIFE* THANOS PROMISED YOU.

HIS *DEATH* HAS FREED YOU TO DO SO.

KAFF!

KOFF! KAFF! KOFF!

MAR-VELL, ARE YOU ALL RIGHT?

KAFF! KOFF!

I DIDN'T SEE ANYONE LAY A HAND ON HIM DURING THE BATTLE...?

I DON'T THINK ANYONE DID.

I'M... I'M ALL RIGHT... NOW.

WHAT HAPPENED TO YOU?

...JUST A LITTLE... WINDED.

LET'S GET THANOS ON BACK TO TITAN!

MAR-VELL, I'D LIKE TO RUN YOU THROUGH A MEDI-SCAN ON THE COMPUTER ISAAC WHEN WE RETURN HOME.

ANY OBJECTIONS?

NO... BUT I'M AFRAID ISAAC WILL ONLY BE ABLE TO CONFIRM WHAT I ALREADY SUSPECT.

WHAT DO YOU MEAN?

YOU FORGET MY POWER.

COSMIC AWARE-NESS CAN BE TURNED INWARD.

MY BODY HAS NO SECRETS I CAN-NOT UNRAVEL.

THEN THERE IS SOMETHING WRONG?

PERHAP'S ISAAC'S MEDI-CENTER CAN BE OF SOME AID?

PERHAPS... BUT I DOUBT IT.

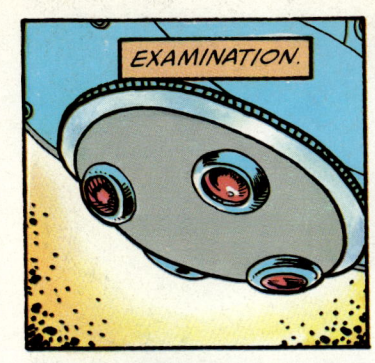

EXAMINATION.

ANALYZATION.

COMPUTATION.

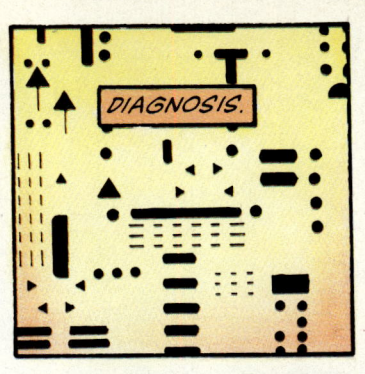

DIAGNOSIS.

YOU WERE RIGHT. ISAAC CONFIRMS THE FINDINGS OF YOUR COSMIC SENSES.

I'M SORRY...

I WAS SURE MY SENSES WERE RIGHT. I DETECTED THE DISEASE A COUPLE OF WEEKS AGO.

I'VE STUDIED A MOUNTAIN OF MEDICAL VOLUMES, SEARCHING FOR A CURE FOR MY PARTICULAR PROBLEM ...AND FAILED.

I'VE NOT ASKED FOR YOUR HELP BEFORE BECAUSE I'VE BEEN UN-ABLE TO VOICE MY FEAR.

I CAN UNDERSTAND THAT... IT'S A TERRIBLE DISEASE.

WE, ON TITAN, CALL IT THE INNER DECAY.

YOU KREE HAVE NAMED IT THE BLACKEND.

EARTHMEN CALL IT CANCER.

ISAAC ALSO GIVES A *NEGATIVE* PROGNOSIS.

BUT WE ON TITAN HAVE HAD VERY *LITTLE EXPERIENCE* WITH THIS PROBLEM. OUR ENVIRONMENT IS VERY UNPOLLUTED...

HOW MUCH *TIME* DOES ISAAC GIVE ME?

ABOUT *THREE MONTHS*...I JUST CAN'T UNDERSTAND HOW THIS COULD HAPPEN TO YOU.

IT WAS ABOUT SEVEN YEARS AGO... I WAS BACK ON *EARTH*...

THERE WAS THIS THIEF CALLED *NITRO* WHO HAD STOLEN A CANISTER OF *NERVE GAS* FROM THE UNITED STATES ARMY.

DURING OUR BATTLE, THE GAS CANISTER BROKE OPEN AND ITS DEADLY CONTENTS THREATENED THE LIVES OF *THOUSANDS* WHO LIVED IN THE AREA.

I HAD NO CHOICE. I HAD TO RESEAL THE TANK WITH MY *BARE HANDS.*

I REALIZE NOW THE NERVE GAS ACTED AS A *CARCINOGEN* IN MY BODY. THE MOMENT IT TOUCHED ME I BEGAN TO DIE.

IN FACT I PROBABLY SHOULD HAVE DIED *YEARS* AGO.

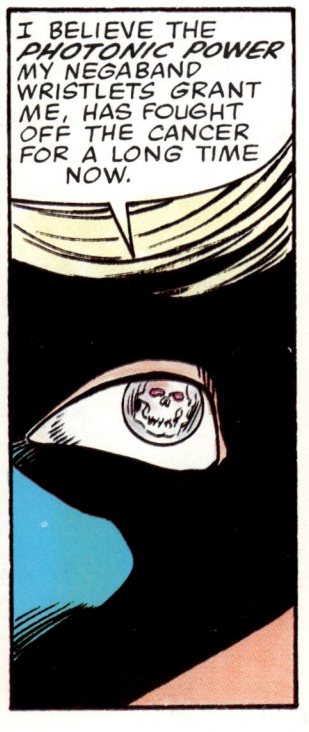

I BELIEVE THE *PHOTONIC POWER* MY NEGABAND WRISTLETS GRANT ME, HAS FOUGHT OFF THE CANCER FOR A LONG TIME NOW.

BUT THE *REMISSION PERIOD* IS OVER. THE DISEASE RESUMES ITS MARCH TO DARKNESS.

I...WE OF TITAN WILL DO ANYTHING WE CAN TO HELP YOU.

WHATEVER YOU NEED...

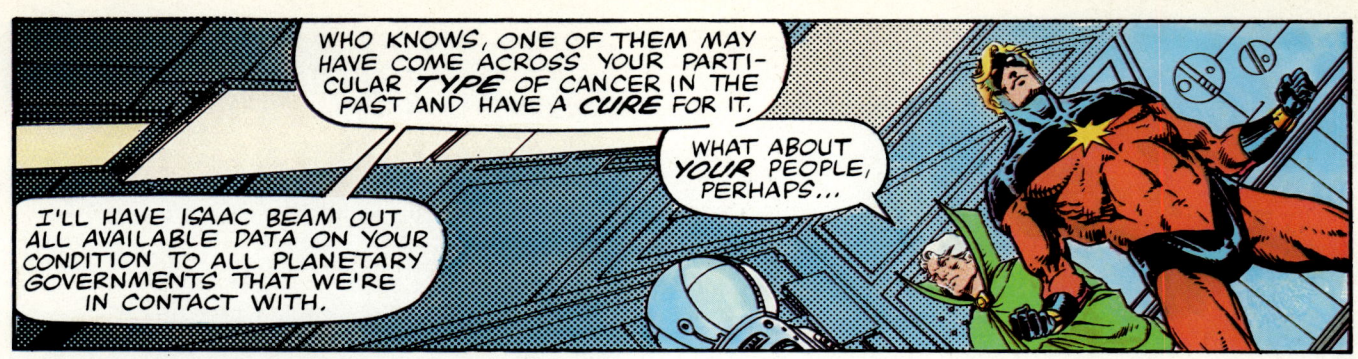

WHO KNOWS, ONE OF THEM MAY HAVE COME ACROSS YOUR PARTICULAR *TYPE* OF CANCER IN THE PAST AND HAVE A *CURE* FOR IT.

WHAT ABOUT *YOUR* PEOPLE, PERHAPS...

I'LL HAVE ISAAC BEAM OUT ALL AVAILABLE DATA ON YOUR CONDITION TO ALL PLANETARY GOVERNMENTS THAT WE'RE IN CONTACT WITH.

NO, *WAR* HAS ALWAYS BEEN THE KREE EMPIRE'S CHIEF PREOCCUPATION.

THEY'VE NEVER HAD THE SPARE *TIME* OR *RESOURCES* NEEDED TO FIND A CURE FOR THE *BLACKEND.*

THEY'RE A LOT LIKE *EARTH* IN THAT RESPECT.

HAVE YOU ANY PLANS? I MEAN...

TERMINAL DISEASE FIGHTING IS A LITTLE OUT OF MY LEAGUE.

I'M A *WARRIOR* NOT A *DOCTOR.*

ALL I CAN DO IS HOPE... *PRAY* THAT YOU AND ISSAC CAN HELP ME.

BUT DON'T WORRY, I'M NOT EXPECTING *MIRACLES* FROM YOU.

I'D *WELCOME* ONE, BUT I DON'T EXPECT ANY.

I FIGURE MY TIME HAS COME AT LAST. I NEVER EXPECTED IT TO BE LIKE THIS, BUT...

...I'M LEARNING TO... LIVE WITH IT.

DOES *ELYSIUS* KNOW?

NO...
NOT
YET.

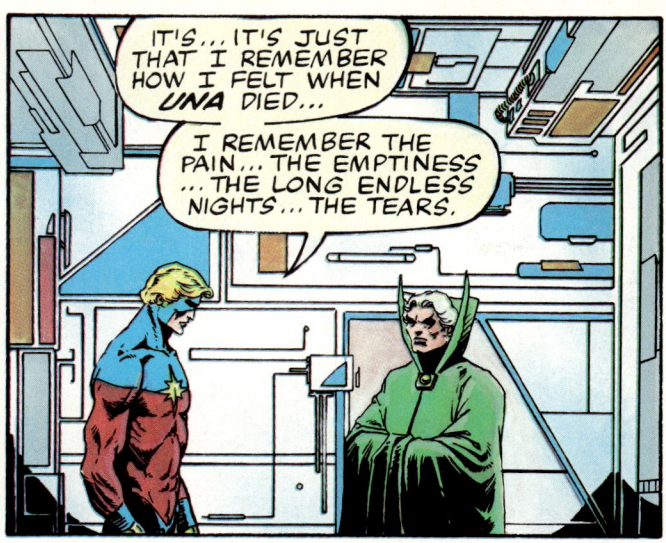

IT'S...IT'S JUST THAT I REMEMBER HOW I FELT WHEN UNA DIED...

I REMEMBER THE PAIN...THE EMPTINESS ...THE LONG ENDLESS NIGHTS...THE TEARS.

THIS IS NOT THE LEGACY I WISH TO LEAVE ELYSIUS. I WAS HOPING SOMETHING WOULD POP UP OR THAT I'D WAKE UP AND FIND IT WAS ALL A BAD DREAM...

BUT MIRACLES AND MIRACLE CURES ARE THE FOOD OF FOOLS, RIDICULOUS OPIATES THAT BLIND ONE TO HIS DUTIES AND RESPONSIBILITIES.

YOU WILL EXCUSE ME, MENTOR. I HAVE THINGS I MUST TAKE CARE OF.

DAMN MY STARS! I WISH I'D LEARN TO KEEP MY EVER-QUESTIONING MOUTH SHUT.

I CAN'T THINK OF ANY HAPPIER COUPLE THAN THOSE TWO.

ELYSIUS HAS FILLED THE GAP AND HEALED THE WOUND WHICH UNA'S DEATH LEFT IN MAR-VELL'S SOUL...

...AND THAT KREE WARRIOR HAS QUIETED THE SECRET TURMOIL WHICH USED TO HAUNT ELYSIUS'S EYES.

SURELY THE STARS ORDAINED THEIR LOVE. NEVER HAVE TWO PEOPLE COMPLIMENTED OR NEEDED EACH OTHER MORE.

COULD THE FATES BE SO CRUEL AS TO END THEIR LOVE IN SUCH A WAY.

I PRAY NOT.

BELOW, IN THE ROYAL GARDENS.

CAPTAIN MARVEL HERE AGAIN -- AND THIS IS *AUTOBIO TAPE #2* FOR AVENGERS' FILES.

BY HALA, HOW DO YOU PUT YOUR ENTIRE LIFE INTO A FEW HOURS OF TAPE?

YOU CAN'T.

ALL YOU CAN DO IS TALK AND HOPE THAT WHAT YOU'RE SAYING WILL MEAN SOMETHING TO SOMEONE, SOMEWHERE, SOMEDAY.

NOW, WHERE WAS I...? YES... I HAD DESERTED THE KREE EMPIRE...

...BUT LESS THAN A YEAR LATER I WAS *TRICKED* INTO RETURNING TO *KREE-LAR*, CAPITAL OF THE KREE GALAXY.

THERE I STOOD, BEFORE THE EMPIRE'S ALL-POWERFUL MONARCH...

...THE *SUPREME INTELLIGENCE.*

BUT I DIDN'T STAND THERE FOR LONG.

THE FIEND TELEPORTED ME OFF TO A STRANGE DIMENSION CALLED THE *NEGATIVE ZONE.*

IT SEEMED I WAS *DOOMED* TO SPEND THE REST OF MY LIFE FLOATING IN THAT COSMIC *WASTELAND...*

...AND I *WOULD* HAVE, IF IT HADN'T BEEN FOR THE EARTH YOUTH NAMED *RICK JONES.*

FOR RICK FOUND, WITHIN A SECRET CAVERN, THE ANCIENT *NEGA-BANDS* OF THE KREE.

WE FOUND THAT ONCE RICK PUT THE BANDS ON, HE AND I COULD **COMMUNICATE** ACROSS THAT VAST DIMENSIONAL GAP.

BUT EVEN **BETTER** THAN THAT WAS THE DISCOVERY THAT IF RICK SLAPPED THE WRISTLETS TOGETHER, AN EVEN STRANGER INTERCHANGE WAS POSSIBLE.

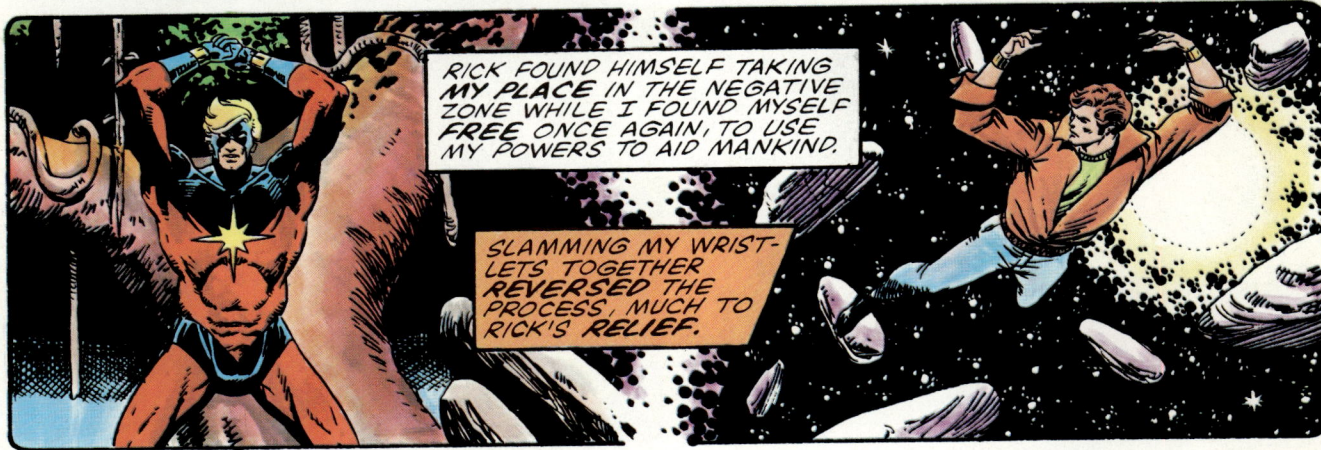

RICK FOUND HIMSELF TAKING **MY PLACE** IN THE NEGATIVE ZONE WHILE I FOUND MYSELF **FREE** ONCE AGAIN, TO USE MY POWERS TO AID MANKIND.

SLAMMING MY WRIST-LETS TOGETHER **REVERSED** THE PROCESS, MUCH TO RICK'S **RELIEF.**

IT WAS DURING ONE OF MY EARLY **LEAVES** FROM THE NEGATIVE ZONE THAT I AT LAST CAUGHT UP WITH **YON-ROGG** AND MADE HIM PAY FOR **UNA'S** MURDER.

FINALLY, MY KREE PAST WAS COMPLETELY BEHIND ME. TRUE, MY NEW LIFE, SHARING **TIME** AND **SPACE** WITH AN EARTH TEENAGER, WAS A BIT HARD TO GET USED TO.

BUT OUR STRANGE RELATIONSHIP ALLOWED ME TO LEARN SO MANY THINGS ABOUT MY NEW HOME, EARTH, THAT I WOULD HAVE NEVER REALIZED **ALONE.**

RICK AND I BECAME CLOSE **FRIENDS.**

BUT RICK WASN'T THE ONLY EARTHLING I CAME TO KNOW. THERE WERE ALSO THE **AVENGERS.**

I **USUALLY** WORKED ALONE, BUT OCCASIONALLY, I FOUND MYSELF FIGHTING BY THEIR SIDE-- AND I'M GLAD I DID.

THEY PROVED TO BE GOOD **COMRADES** AND THE STARS ONLY KNOW HOW MANY TIMES WE NEEDED EACH OTHERS' HELP.

IT'S A DARK UNIVERSE OUT THERE WITH MANY A **DANGER** AND NEARLY AS MANY **ENEMIES.**

SOME LATER
BECAME FRIENDS,
BUT TOO FEW...

I'M AFRAID I'M GOING TO LEAVE BEHIND
ME MORE ENEMIES THAN ANY MAN
SHOULD HAVE HAD IN ONE LIFETIME.

BUT THE ONE FOE I'M *GLAD* I STOOD AGAINST ALSO PROVED TO BE THE MOST FORMIDABLE... THE *MAD WARLORD OF TITAN, THANOS.*

HE WORSHIPPED *DEATH* AND WISHED TO SACRIFICE ALL LIFE IN THIS UNIVERSE AS A LOVE OFFERING TO HIS *DARK MISTRESS.*

HE BEGAN WITH AN INTERGALACTIC ARMY OF THRALLS. THEN THERE WAS THAT MASSIVE *MIND CONTROL* EXPERIMENT AND THE *COSMIC CUBE* AND SO MANY OTHER SCHEMES AND PLANS.

IT WAS USUALLY *ADAM WARLOCK* OR MYSELF THAT THWARTED HIS INSANE PLOTS. BUT NEARLY EVERY EARTH SUPER HERO BECAME ENMESHED IN HIS NETWORK OF SCHEMES AT ONE TIME OR ANOTHER.

IN THE END, IT TOOK NEARLY ALL OF US TO STOP HIM.

NOW THANOS *RESTS* IN A SUB-BASEMENT TOMB OF THIS PALACE AND THE UNIVERSE *SLEEPS* EASIER AT NIGHT.

BUT I WAS TALKING ABOUT RICK, WASN'T I...?

SHORTLY AFTER THE THANOS AFFAIR, I WAS ABLE TO *ESCAPE* FROM THE *NEGATIVE ZONE.*

WE WENT OUR SEPARATE WAYS THEN. RICK LEFT TO PURSUE HIS *MUSIC CAREER* AND I RETURNED TO THE ONLY LIFE I'VE EVER KNOWN, THAT OF THE *WARRIOR.*

IT'S BEEN A COUPLE OF YEARS SINCE I'VE SEEN RICK. I WANTED TO LET HIM GET HIS LIFE TOGETHER WITHOUT MY SHADOW GETTING IN HIS WAY.

BUT I REALIZE NOW, THAT I MUST LOCATE AND TALK TO HIM AS SOON AS POSSIBLE.

HIS *LIFE* MAY *DEPEND* ON IT.

EARTH... NEW YORK CITY. THE NIGHT SPRING AIR IS COOL AND REFRESHING.

JUST RIGHT FOR SITTING ON A 44TH STREET TENEMENT ROOF.

THE GUITAR'S GENTLE RHYTHMS WEAVE SAD PATTERNS...

... AND A STRONG BUT SENSUOUS VOICE FILLS THE TWILIGHT BREEZES WITH SONGS THAT SEEM STRANGE COMING FROM ONE SO YOUNG. YET EVEN A SHORT LIFE CAN BE RICH WITH EXPERIENCE...

ESPECIALLY IF THAT LIFE BELONGS TO...

RICK JONES.

WHO?

CAP!

YOU KNOW, I THINK YOU'VE ACTUALLY GOTTEN BETTER SINCE THE LAST TIME I HEARD YOU SING AND YOU WERE TERRIFIC THEN.

BOY, IT'S GOOD TO SEE YOU, MARV!

HOW YOU DOING?

NOT SO WELL, RICK. IN FACT, THAT'S WHAT I'VE COME TO SEE YOU ABOUT.

I WANT YOU TO HEAD OVER TO *AVENGERS' MANSION* TOMORROW MORNING. I'VE ARRANGED FOR A *DR. BLAKE* TO GIVE YOU A COMPLETE PHYSICAL CHECK-UP.

CHECK-UP?

DON'T TELL ME YOU'VE COME ALL THE WAY FROM *TITAN* JUST TO MAKE SURE I'M TAKING CARE OF MY *HEALTH*?

WHAT'S GOING ON HERE, MARV?

REMEMBER BACK WHEN WE WERE *SHARING* BODIES AND WE HAD A RUN-IN WITH THAT LUNATIC LEGIONNAIRE, *NITRO*?

SURE.

I ALSO REMEMBER THAT LEAKING CANISTER OF *NERVE GAS.* THAT WAS REALLY A CLOSE SHAVE.

CLOSER THAN YOU THINK, RICK.

YOU'LL RECALL I WAS *EXPOSED* TO THAT GAS. OVER THE YEARS, THAT GAS HAS *AFFECTED* ME.

AFFECTED YOU...? *HOW*?

I'VE GOT *CANCER*, RICK, AND IT'S *INOPERABLE.*

I'VE LESS THAN FOUR MONTHS TO LIVE.

CANCER... IT CAN'T BE...

BUT IT IS. THAT'S WHY I WANT YOU TO GET THIS CHECK UP.

I DON'T THINK OUR *SYMBIOTIC RELATIONSHIP* WOULD ALLOW THIS DISEASE TO BE PASSED ON TO YOU, BUT WE SHOULDN'T TAKE ANY CHANCES.

IS THIS SOME KIND OF JOKE?

I WISH IT WERE...

BUT WHAT ABOUT YOU? YOU'RE GETTING SOME KIND OF *TREATMENT*, AREN'T YOU?

YES, MENTOR HAS BEGUN GIVING ME *RADIATION* TREATMENTS...

...AND IF THOSE FAIL, HE'S DEVISED A FORM OF *CHEMOTHERAPY* FOR ME TO TRY.

BUT THE TROUBLE IS... I'M A *KREE.*

MY *BIOLOGICAL SYSTEM* IS DIFFERENT THAN SOMEONE FROM *TITAN* OR *EARTH.*

BECAUSE OF THIS, IS AC ONLY GIVES ME A .09 PERCENT CHANCE FOR RECOVERY WITHOUT HELP FROM *KREE* MEDICAL SCIENTISTS...

...AND THE KREE EMPIRE IS *NOT* ABOUT TO HELP SAVE THE LIFE OF ONE THEY CONSIDER A *TRAITOR.*

I'M AFRAID IT DOESN'T LOOK TOO GOOD FOR ME.

SO YOU'RE JUST GOING TO *GIVE UP* AND *DIE?*

RICK!

DON'T GIVE ME THIS *'NO HOPE'* CRAP!

YOU FORGET I'VE SEEN YOU IN ACTION.

YOU'VE BEEN IN TIGHT SCRAPES BEFORE, FACED IMPOSSIBLE ODDS, BUT YOU'VE ALWAYS COME OUT ON TOP.

WITH YOUR *PHOTONIC POWERS* AND *COSMIC SENSES* YOU CAN BEAT ANYTHING.

YOU'RE A *KREE WARRIOR,* TRAINED TO FIGHT DEATH, NOT LAY DOWN AND *SURRENDER* TO IT.

I'M AFRAID ALL MY POWERS ARE *USELESS* IN THIS SITUATION, RICK.

I CAN'T PUNCH, KICK OR FLY AWAY TO ESCAPE THIS CANCER. IT JUST DOESN'T WORK THAT WAY.

IT'S *MY BODY* THAT'S BETRAYED ME. IT'S MY *OWN BIOLOGY* WHICH IS KILLING ME.

THERE'S *NOTHING* MY POWERS CAN DO TO SAVE ME.

ALL THEY CAN DO IS HELP ME TO *ACCEPT* MY FATE.

ACCEPT...

WELL MAYBE *YOU'RE* PREPARED TO ACCEPT IT, BUT I'M *NOT!*

MAYBE **YOU'RE** WILLING TO GIVE UP ON LIVING, BUT I'M **NOT**.

YOU'RE **PART** OF MY **LIFE!** I'M NOT GOING TO QUIETLY SIT BY AND **WATCH** YOU **DIE!**

I'M **NOT** GOING TO LET YOU **DIE!**

RICK...

THERE'S GOT TO BE **SOMEWAY** TO BEAT THIS...

...AND I'M **GOING** TO **FIND** IT!

RICK! WAIT!

SLAM!

RICK...

RICK...

...I'M SORRY. I CAN'T HELP IT.

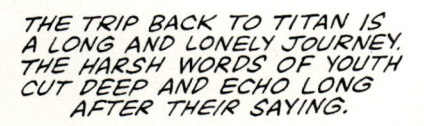

THE TRIP BACK TO TITAN IS A LONG AND LONELY JOURNEY. THE HARSH WORDS OF YOUTH CUT DEEP AND ECHO LONG AFTER THEIR SAYING.

FORTUNATELY, ONE AWAITS HIS RETURN IN THE ROYAL GARDEN.

I JUST DON'T UNDERSTAND HIM.

HE WAS SO **ANGRY**, AS IF HE WERE MAD AT **ME** FOR HAVING CANCER.

RICK'S AN **ORPHAN**, ISN'T HE?

OF COURSE...ALL HIS LIFE PEOPLE HAVE BEEN *LEAVING* HIM BEHIND.

FIRST HIS *PARENTS* DIED. THEN FOR AWHILE HE WAS PARTNERS WITH THE *HULK* AND LATER *CAPTAIN AMERICA.*

NEITHER TEAM EVER REALLY WORKED OUT.

NOW *I'M* LEAVING HIM BEHIND TOO...

...POOR RICK.

I GUESS IT REALLY IS HARDER ON THOSE YOU LEAVE BEHIND.

I'M SORRY, ELYSIUS.

SO AM I, MAR.

COME SIT AWHILE.

YOU KNOW, I'VE BEEN THINKING A LOT LATELY OF ALL THE PEOPLE I'VE MET IN MY LIFETIME.

I'VE MADE QUITE A FEW FRIENDS ALONG THE WAY.

I ALSO KEEP REMEMBERING *ADAM WARLOCK.* I WAS WITH HIM WHEN HE DIED.

HIS WAS A HARD AND SAD LIFE, FILLED WITH PAIN AND CONFUSION.

WHEN DEATH CAME FOR HIM HE WELCOMED IT AS A FRIEND.

I'LL NOT DO SO.

I'VE ENJOYED THIS LIFE. IT'S HAD ITS *BAD MOMENTS* BUT IT'S HAD FAR MORE *GOOD MOMENTS.*

I'M GOING TO MISS IT.

HALF A SOLAR SYSTEM AWAY... EARTH.

ONCE AGAIN *NEW YORK CITY*, ONLY THIS TIME THE SETTING IS AN IMPRESSIVE MANHATTAN MANSION OWNED BY *TONY STARK*.

BUT MOST PEOPLE DON'T THINK OF IT AS BEING THE PROPERTY OF THE WEALTHY INDUSTRIALIST. NO, TO THEM IT'S SIMPLY KNOWN AS *AVENGERS' MANSION*.

...THAT'S WHY I ASKED YOU PARTICULAR AVENGERS HERE. YOU SEVEN... YELLOWJACKET, THE BLACK PANTHER, VISION, WONDER MAN, BEAST, IRON MAN, AND THOR, ALL HAVE *SPECIAL SCIENTIFIC* OR *MEDICAL KNOWLEDGE*.

I FIGURE IF ANYONE CAN SAVE CAPTAIN MARVEL'S LIFE, *YOU* CAN.

WITH YOUR POWERS AND BRAINS YOU SHOULD BE ABLE TO FIND A *CURE* FOR *CANCER* IN NO TIME AT ALL.

NOW HOLD ON A MINUTE, RICK.

I DON'T THINK YOU UNDERSTAND THE *COMPLEXITIES* OF CANCER RESEARCH. THIS IS A PROBLEM *HUNDREDS* OF RESEARCH SCIENTISTS HAVE BEEN WORKING ON FOR *DECADES*.

IT'S TRUE WE'RE *GOOD* AT WHAT WE DO, BUT CANCER RESEARCH IS SOMETHING COMPLETELY *NEW* TO US.

WHAT I THINK THE BEAST IS TRYING TO SAY IS: '*DON'T* EXPECT ANY *MIRACLES*.' AFTER ALL WE'RE ONLY HUMAN...

...WELL AT LEAST MOST OF US ARE.

OH... I SEE... I GET IT...

IN OTHER WORDS YOU'D LIKE TO HELP...

...BUT IT'S NOT GOOD BUSINESS TAKING ON ANYTHING IT DOESN'T LOOK LIKE YOU CAN LICK...

...BAD FOR THE OLD REPUTATION.

RICK! WAIT! YOU DON'T UNDERSTAND!

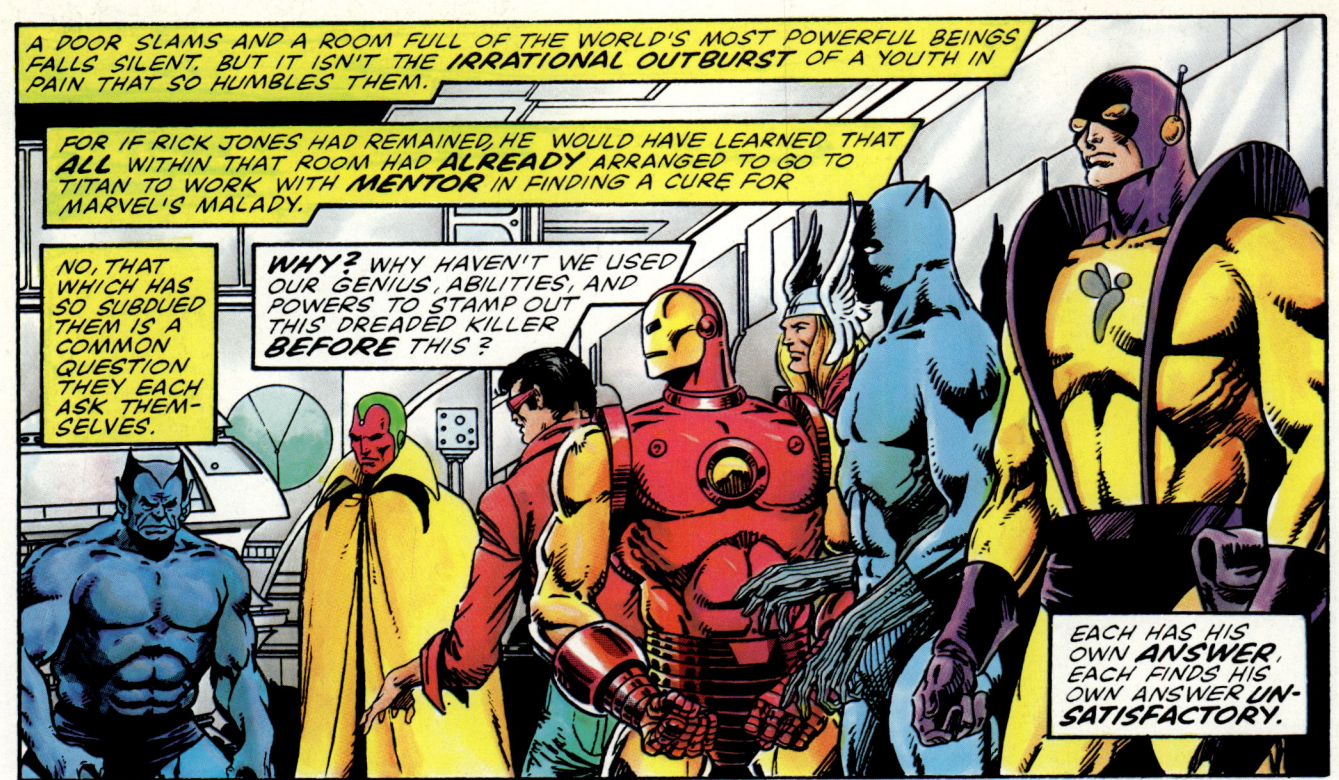

A DOOR SLAMS AND A ROOM FULL OF THE WORLD'S MOST POWERFUL BEINGS FALLS SILENT. BUT IT ISN'T THE *IRRATIONAL OUTBURST* OF A YOUTH IN PAIN THAT SO HUMBLES THEM.

FOR IF RICK JONES HAD REMAINED, HE WOULD HAVE LEARNED THAT *ALL* WITHIN THAT ROOM HAD *ALREADY* ARRANGED TO GO TO TITAN TO WORK WITH *MENTOR* IN FINDING A CURE FOR MARVEL'S MALADY.

NO, THAT WHICH HAS SO SUBDUED THEM IS A COMMON QUESTION THEY EACH ASK THEMSELVES.

WHY? WHY HAVEN'T WE USED OUR GENIUS, ABILITIES, AND POWERS TO STAMP OUT THIS DREADED KILLER *BEFORE* THIS?

EACH HAS HIS OWN *ANSWER*, EACH FINDS HIS OWN ANSWER *UNSATISFACTORY.*

THE DAYS TURN INTO WEEKS AND THE WORD SPREADS THROUGHOUT THE GALAXY...A HERO IS DYING. ONCE AGAIN THE DARKNESS CLAIMS THE LIGHT. THE UNIVERSE IS SOON TO BE A LITTLE EMPTIER.

THE NEWS IS RECEIVED WITH MIXED FEELINGS.

SHOCK AND DISMAY...

JOYOUS TRIUMPH...

RESTRAINED PASSIVITY...

SOME REMEMBER HIM AS A FRIEND--

--TO OTHERS HE WAS A COMRADE.

STILL TO OTHERS, HE MEANT EVEN MORE.

BUT *ALL* FEEL THE LOSS...

...FOR HE IS *CAPTAIN MARVEL.*

ISAAC HAS BEEN RECEIVING DATA TRANSMISSIONS FROM ALL OVER THE GALAXY, MANY WORLDS HAVE FOUND A WAY TO *BEAT* THIS KILLER, *CANCER.*

BUT ISAAC HAS BEEN EXAMINING AND TESTING EACH CURE AS IT COMES IN AND HAS FOUND *NONE* OF THEM CAN HELP *MY* PARTICULAR CASE, RIGHT?

YES, BUT EVERY BIT OF DATA WE GET IS ANOTHER *STEP* TOWARD FINDING A WAY TO HELP *YOU.*

WITHOUT THE AID OF THESE TRANSMISSIONS ISAAC WOULDN'T HAVE BEEN ABLE TO DESIGN THAT *LIFE SUPPORT TUNIC* YOU'VE GOT ON.

THE *MEDI-SYSTEM* BUILT INTO THAT TUNIC HAS REDUCED THE DEGENERATION PROCESS BY SOME *20%.*

YES I KNOW...

...PLUS IT'S GIVEN ME AN EXCUSE TO GET OUT OF MY OLD RED AND BLUE LEOTARD.

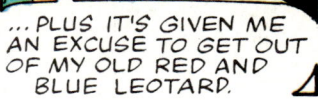

I'M AFRAID I'VE LOST TOO MUCH WEIGHT TO LOOK ANYTHING BUT *SILLY* IN IT.

THINK I'LL WANDER DOWN TO THE *COM-CENTER.*

I'VE SOME TAPES TO RECORD.

EROS!

I'M GLAD I RAN INTO YOU. I'VE BEEN WANTING TO ASK SOMETHING OF YOU.

SURE, WHAT DO YOU NEED?

SOMEONE I CAN *DEPEND* ON.

I'VE KNOWN FOR A LONG TIME HOW YOU FEEL ABOUT *ELYSIUS.*

MAR-VELL... I...I NEVER...

I KNOW, EROS, AND IT'S NOT IMPORTANT NOW. CHANCES ARE THAT IN A SHORT TIME I'LL BE GONE...*DEAD...*

ELYSIUS IS GOING TO NEED SOMEONE SHE CAN TALK TO, CONFIDE IN, TRUST.

SHE IS GOING TO NEED A *FRIEND*.

I CAN'T THINK OF ANY- ONE WHO WOULD BE BETTER AT THAT THAN *YOU*.

WILL YOU...?

...OF COURSE.

THANKS.

ELYSIUS...SHE WAS THE ENEMY I LEARNED TO LOVE.

WHEN WE FIRST MET, ELYSIUS WAS PART OF A MAD DOOMS- DAY LEGACY LEFT BEHIND BY *THANOS*.

HER JOB WAS TO KILL *DRAX* THE DESTROYER AND *MYSELF*.

FORTUNATELY I WAS ABLE TO REACH OUT TO HER, CONVINCE HER THAT SHE SHOULD JOIN FORCES WITH US.

WITH HER HELP WE WERE ABLE TO THWART THE EVIL PLANS OF HER PARTNERS, THE VILLAINOUS *CHAOS* AND *STELLARAX*.

IT WAS ONLY A MATTER OF TIME BEFORE OUR LOVE SURFACED.

WE TOURED EARTH TOGETHER. IT WAS A *HONEYMOON* OF SORTS. I LOVED HER MORE WITH EVERY PASSING DAY. I NEVER KNEW SUCH HAPPINESS.

WE FINALLY DECIDED TO SETTLE DOWN HERE ON TITAN. WE MADE *PLANS* AND TALKED OF HAVING *CHILDREN.*

BUT NOW OUR PLANS ARE *YESTERDAY'S DREAMS* AND OUR CHILDREN ARE WHAT MIGHT HAVE BEEN.

FOR DEATH IS KNOCKING AT MY DOOR AND NOT ALL MY POWER CAN KEEP HIM OUT.

IT WOULD HAVE BEEN A GOOD LIFE, ELYSIUS.

I'M SORRY.

I WISH...

ARH!

PAIN...

OVERWHELMING PAIN...

IT BURNS... IT TEARS... IT TWISTS AND BENDS... IT KILLS.

IT KILLS SLOWLY... A LITTLE PIECE AT A TIME... AND THEN IT FADES.

YES, THE PAIN COMES AND IT GOES...

DAMN!

...BUT THE ANGER ALWAYS REMAINS.

ALIEN INVADERS, SUPER-VILLAINS, MONSTERS, MUTANTS, THEY *ALL* TRIED, BUT *NONE* OF THEM COULD KILL ME.

I SURVIVED!

I FOUGHT THEM ALL AND I WON!

WHO WOULD HAVE THOUGHT THAT, IN THE END...

...IT'D BE MY *OWN BODY* THAT WOULD TURN ON ME AND DO ME IN.

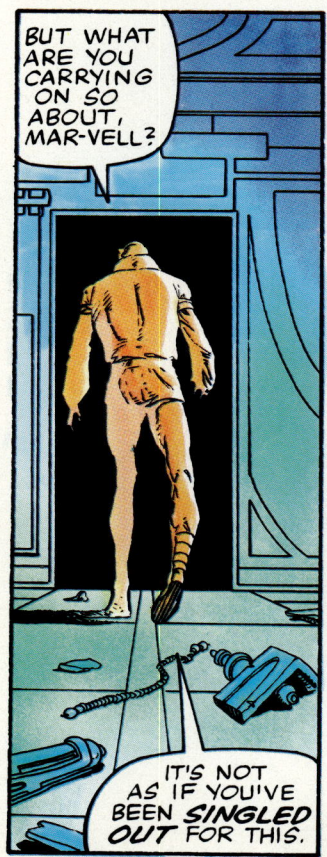

BUT WHAT ARE YOU CARRYING ON SO ABOUT, MAR-VELL?

IT'S NOT AS IF YOU'VE BEEN *SINGLED OUT* FOR THIS.

EVERYONE HAS TO DIE SOMEDAY.

OR DID YOU THINK YOU WERE *UNIQUE?*

YES, I GUESS THAT'S WHAT IT'S ALL ABOUT.

I JUST NEVER FIGURED IT WOULD HAPPEN TO *ME.*

DEEP DOWN INSIDE ME I FELT THAT THOSE *SPECIAL THINGS* THAT MAKE ME WHO I AM WOULD JUST LIVE *FOREVER.*

IT'S HARD TO *ACCEPT* THAT THE WORLD IS GOING TO GO ON *WITHOUT* ME.

DAMN.

IT JUST CAN'T END LIKE THIS, NOT FOR *HIM.*

I WON'T LET IT!

I... WE ON TITAN... EVERYONE IN THE UNIVERSE, WE ALL OWE HIM SO MUCH... WE OWE HIM OUR VERY LIVES A DOZEN TIMES OVER.

I MUST REPAY THAT DEBT TO HIM... AT LEAST *ONCE.*

HOW'S IT GOING IN HERE?

NOT WELL, I FEAR.

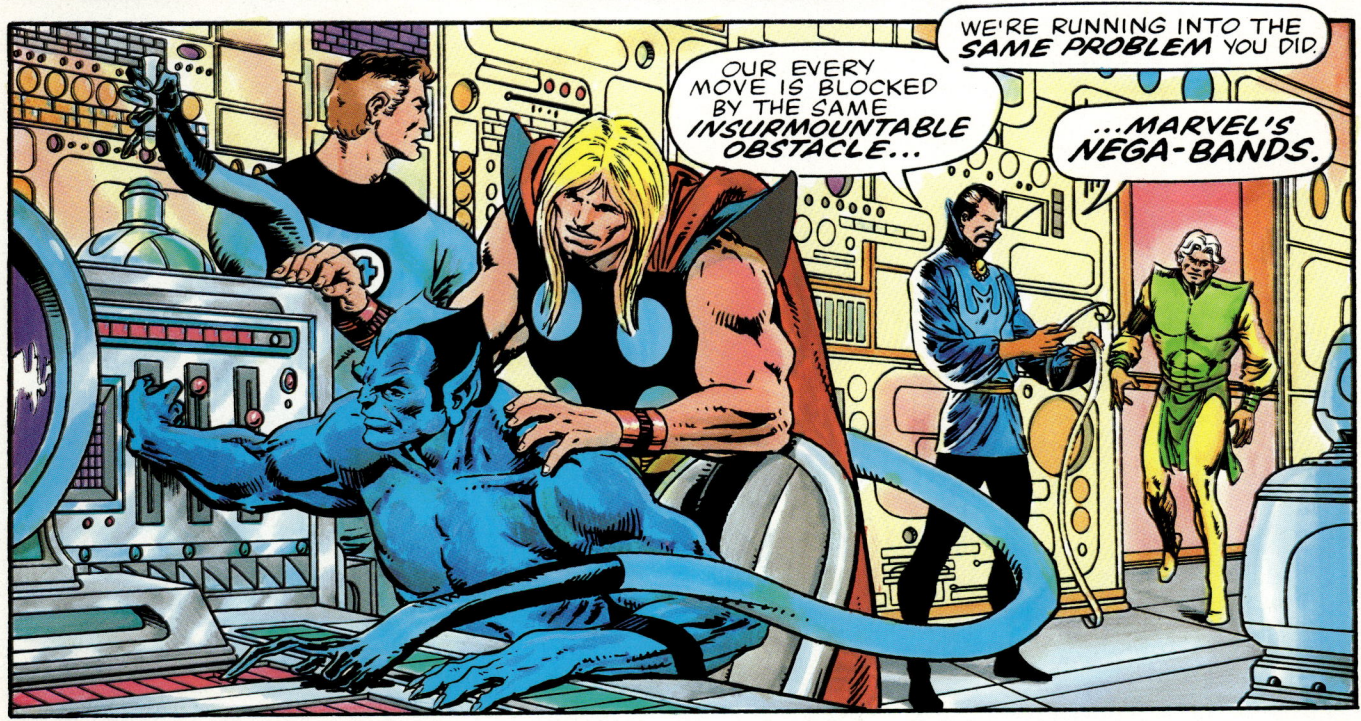

OUR EVERY MOVE IS BLOCKED BY THE SAME *INSURMOUNTABLE OBSTACLE...*

WE'RE RUNNING INTO THE *SAME PROBLEM* YOU DID.

...MARVEL'S *NEGA-BANDS.*

THESE WRISTLETS CHARGE HIS BODY WITH THE *PHOTONIC ENERGY* THAT KEPT HIS CANCER IN CHECK ALL THESE YEARS.

BUT DURING THAT TIME HIS DISEASE HAS *MUTATED* GAINED AN *IMMUNITY* TO THOSE PHOTONIC ENERGIES.

AS THE CANCER SPREAD, THE CAPTAIN'S BODY CAME TO *DEPEND* MORE AND MORE ON THE *NEGA-BANDS'* POWER TO SUSTAIN LIFE. NOW IT'S GOTTEN TO THE POINT WHERE I DOUBT MARVEL COULD LIVE MORE THAN A *FEW HOURS* WITHOUT THOSE WRISTLETS.

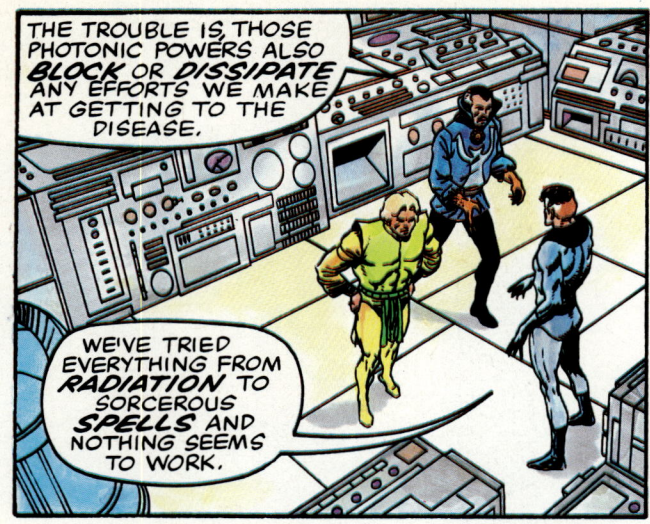

THE TROUBLE IS, THOSE PHOTONIC POWERS ALSO *BLOCK* OR *DISSIPATE* ANY EFFORTS WE MAKE AT GETTING TO THE DISEASE.

WE'VE TRIED EVERYTHING FROM *RADIATION* TO SORCEROUS *SPELLS* AND NOTHING SEEMS TO WORK.

IN OTHER WORDS, THE ONE THING THAT'S KEEPING MARVEL *ALIVE* IS ALSO KEEPING US FROM *CURING* HIM!

FATHER! IT'S *MAR-VELL!*

HE'S *COLLAPSED.* WE'VE TAKEN HIM TO THE EAST WING'S MASTER CHAMBER.

GENTLEMEN, OUR TIME RUNS SHORT.

LET US MAKE EVERY MOMENT COUNT.

MEANWHILE, ON THE FAR SIDE OF THE ROYAL PALACE, DOWN A LONG AND QUIET CORRIDOR AND BEHIND OAK PANELED DOORS...

...A WOMAN SITS WITH HER MAN.

THE LONG HARD VIGIL THAT ALL LOVERS FEAR, BEGINS.

SHE WEEPS.

HE JOINS HER.

BUT HIS TEARS ARE MIXED WITH TUMULTUOUS EMOTIONS THAT HAUNT HIS SLEEP.

TITAN, A MOON OF SATURN, DRIFTS THROUGH SPACE AND WEEKS OF TIME...WAITING.

THEN, ONE DAY, THEY BEGIN TO ARRIVE. THE FIRST SHIPS COME FROM EARTH.

BUT THEY ARE SOON JOINED BY MORE ADVANCED AND EXOTIC ETHER-CUTTERS FROM OUTSIDE OUR SOLAR SYSTEM.

ALL CRAFTS ARE IMMEDIATELY IDENTIFIED AND CLEARED FOR LANDING EXCEPT ONE.

BUT FINALLY, EVEN *THAT* SHIP IS GRANTED CLEARANCE, ONCE CERTAIN GUARANTEES OF PROPER CONDUCT ARE ASSURED BY A PASSENGER ON BOARD.

HOW'S HE HOLDING UP, EROS? ANY CHANCE...?

WELL, AS YOU KNOW, HE'S TOO *FAR* ALONG FOR ANY OPERATION TO DO ANY GOOD...

...AND MY FATHER AND YOUR FRIENDS HAVE HAD *NO LUCK* FINDING AN ALTERNATIVE *CURE.*

SO I'M AFRAID IT'S ONLY A MATTER OF TIME.

BUT I'M SURE HE'LL BE GLAD TO SEE YOU ALL. I THINK HE MISSES EARTH.

NOT HALF AS MUCH AS *EARTH* IS GOING TO MISS *HIM.*

I'LL GO CHECK ON HIM. *ELYSIUS* IS WITH HIM NOW.

...SO AFTER THAT, I JUST DRIFTED AROUND UNTIL I CAME TO TITAN.

YOU KNOW THAT'S THE MOST *FRUSTRATING* PART OF THIS WHOLE BUSINESS OF DEATH.

THERE'S SO MUCH I DON'T KNOW ABOUT YOU AND SO *LITTLE TIME* LEFT ME TO FIND IT ALL OUT.

YES... MUCH TOO SHORT A TIME.

BUT THE TIME WE'VE HAD HAS BEEN GOOD.

I'VE NEVER LOVED ANYONE AS I HAVE YOU.

I FEEL THE SAME, BUT I NEVER DREAMT IT WOULD END LIKE THIS FOR US.

BUT PERHAPS THIS WAY IS BEST.

I ALWAYS FIGURED *YOU* WOULD GO BEFORE *I* DID.

YOUR TYPE OF LIFESTYLE DOESN'T LEND ITSELF TO *LONGEVITY.*

BUT I FEARED YOUR END WOULD BE *VIOLENT.* I DREADED YOU DYING *ALONE* ON SOME DISTANT PLANET SURROUNDED BY ENEMIES.

AT LEAST THIS WAY *I* CAN BE WITH *YOU* TO THE END.

I WANT TO SHARE EVERY MOMENT OF LIFE WITH YOU I CAN SQUEEZE OUT.

I HOPE THAT DOESN'T SOUND TOO *SELFISH.*

NO, NOT AT ALL. I THINK IT'S *BEAUTIFUL.*

EXCUSE ME...

THERE ARE SOME FOLKS FROM *EARTH* WHO WOULD LIKE TO SEE YOU.

ARE YOU UP TO VISITORS?

FROM EARTH?

RICK?

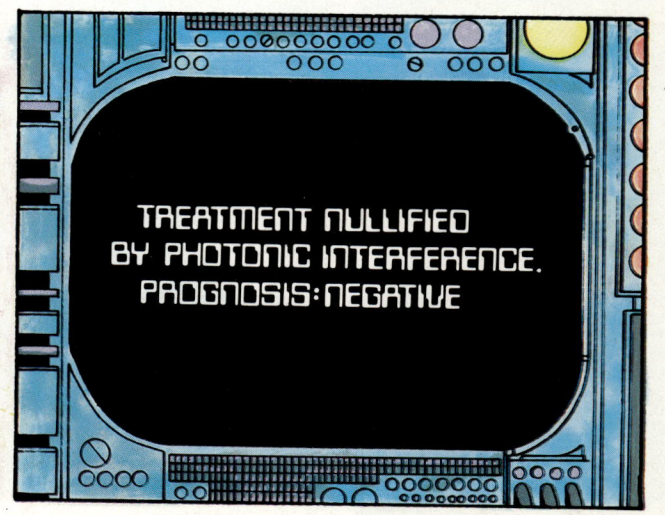

TREATMENT NULLIFIED BY PHOTONIC INTERFERENCE. PROGNOSIS: NEGATIVE

ANOTHER FAILURE...

EVERY AVENUE WE EXPLORE ON ISAAC'S *MEDI-SIMULATOR* IS BLOCKED BY THAT BLASTED *PHOTONIC ENERGY.*

THERE MUST BE SOME WAY TO GET AROUND IT.

YES, BUT *HOW?*

PERHAPS A *COMBINATION* OF TREATMENTS?

MEANWHILE...

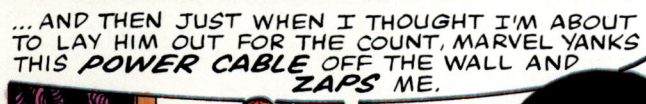

...AND THEN JUST WHEN I THOUGHT I'M ABOUT TO LAY HIM OUT FOR THE COUNT, MARVEL YANKS THIS *POWER CABLE* OFF THE WALL AND *ZAPS* ME.

I TELL YOU, ELYSIUS, THIS IS ONE *TOUGH COOKIE* YOU GOT.

AIN'T THAT RIGHT, SPIDEY?

I...

I... I MEAN... SURE...

PLEASE... EXCUSE ME...

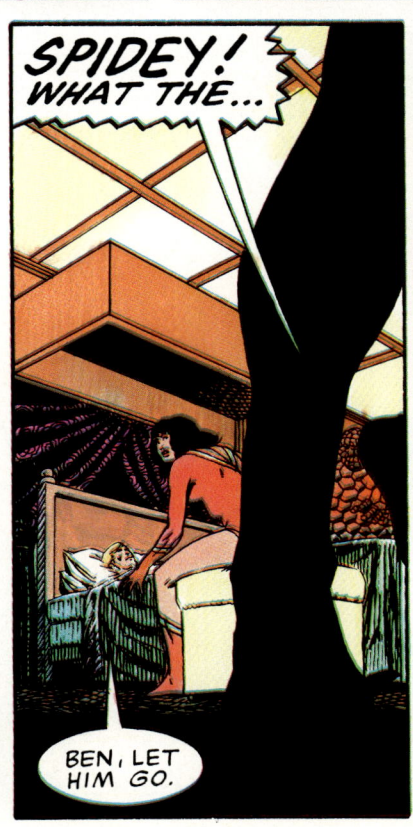

SPIDEY! WHAT THE...

BEN, LET HIM GO.

DEATH TOUCHES US ALL IN *DIFFERENT WAYS.*

SOME BARELY FEEL ITS PASSING.

OTHERS, IT STRIKES RIGHT IN THE *FACE.*

STILL OTHERS FEEL ITS SHARP BLADE IN THEIR *HEARTS.*

SPIDEY, ARE YOU ALL RIGHT?

YEAH SURE... JUST A LITTLE SHAKEN.

IT'S ALL JUST A BIT TOO MUCH.

I MEAN, THIS JUST *CAN'T* BE HAPPENING.

CAPTAIN MARVEL IS ONE OF US. HE'S A FULL-BLOWN, CARD CARRYING *SUPER HERO.*

WE DIE FROM *BULLETS* AND *BOMBS...*

...NOT FROM SOMETHING LIKE *CANCER.* IT JUST CAN'T BE.

I'M AFRAID IT IS.

IN CASE YOU HADN'T NOTICED, BENEATH MOST OF THESE FANCY COSTUMES AND FLASHY POWERS HIDE MORTAL *MEN* AND *WOMEN.*

NONE OF US HAVE MUCH OF A SAY ON HOW WE'RE GOING TO END THIS LIFE.

I GUESS NOT...

BUT DON'T FEEL ALONE IN YOUR FEELINGS, SPIDEY. WE'RE ALL HAVING A HARD TIME ACCEPTING THIS...

...ESPECIALLY *HIM!*

RICK JONES!

HI, GANG! QUITE A LINE-UP TO SEE MARV.

DO I GRAB A NUMBER OR SOMETHING?

NO, YOU JUST WALK RIGHT IN. HE'S BEEN WAITING FOR YOU.

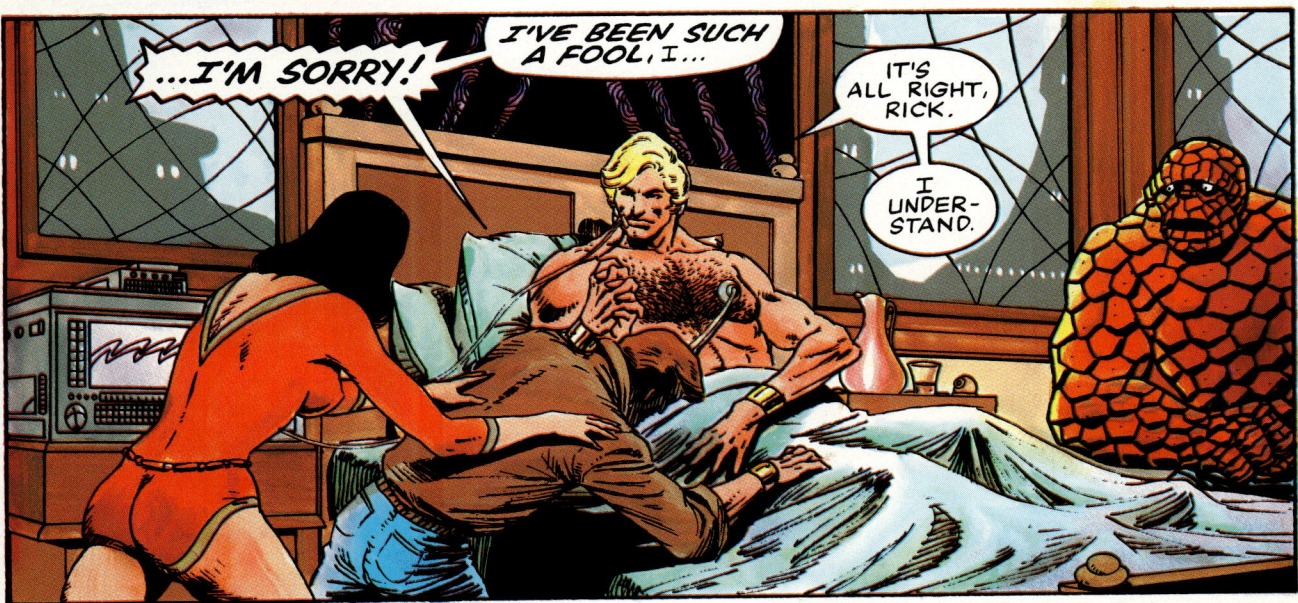

SOMETIME LATER...

HELLO...

...CAN WE COME IN?

DRAX! DRAX THE DESTROYER!

...AND MOON-DRAGON!

BY HALA, DRAX! IT'S BEEN A LONG TIME. HOW HAVE YOU BEEN?

BETTER THAN EVER.

HEATHER... MOONDRAGON AND I HAVE BEEN TRAVELING, GETTING TO KNOW EACH OTHER, LEARNING TO LIVE WITH OUR UNIVERSE.

HOW ARE YOU FARING?

PRETTY WELL CONSIDERING THE CIRCUMSTANCES. THERE'S PAIN AND THAT UNCERTAINTY...

...AND THE FEAR.

AS YOU KNOW I'VE BEEN TO WHERE YOU'RE HEADING.

WE'VE ALL BEEN HANDED A LOT OF GARBAGE THROUGHOUT OUR LIVES ABOUT WHAT DEATH IS LIKE.

NO DESCRIPTION I'VE EVER HEARD COMES EVEN CLOSE.

IT'S INDESCRI-BABLE AND IT'S REALLY NOT ALL THAT BAD.

THANKS, DRAX. BUT YOU'LL FORGIVE ME IF I DON'T RUSH OFF TO FIND OUT IF YOU'RE GIVING IT TO ME STRAIGHT.

OF COURSE, TAKE YOUR TIME.

IN THE MEANTIME I'VE SOMEONE WITH ME WHO WANTS TO MEET YOU.

WHO?

HIM!

CAPTAIN MARVEL, I'D LIKE TO PRESENT TO YOU *GENERAL ZEDRAO.*

IT'S A *SKRULL!*

RICK, YOU CAN PUT THAT BOTTLE DOWN. THE GENERAL IS HERE ON AN OFFICIAL *AFFAIR* OF *STATE.*

HE HAS *ASSURED* ME THAT HIS MISSION IS PEACEFUL AND MY PRESENCE *GUARANTEES* IT.

CAPTAIN MARVEL, I GREET YOU IN THE NAME OF THE *IMPERIAL SKRULL EMPIRE.*

I AM HERE *NOT* BECAUSE YOU ARE OUR *ENEMY* BUT BECAUSE YOU HAVE ALWAYS BEEN OUR *GREATEST* ENEMY.

NO BEING IN THE ENTIRE GALAXY HAS EVER FACED OUR ARMED MIGHT SO *BRAVELY* OR THWARTED OUR PLANS AS MANY TIMES AS *YOU* HAVE.

YOU ARE QUITE POSSIBLY THE *GREATEST WARRIOR* WHO EVER WALKED THE STARS.

WE SKRULLS ARE A *MARTIAL RACE* AND HAVE LONG RESPECTED YOUR SKILLS, DEEDS, AND COURAGE EVEN THOUGH YOU ARE OUR FOE.

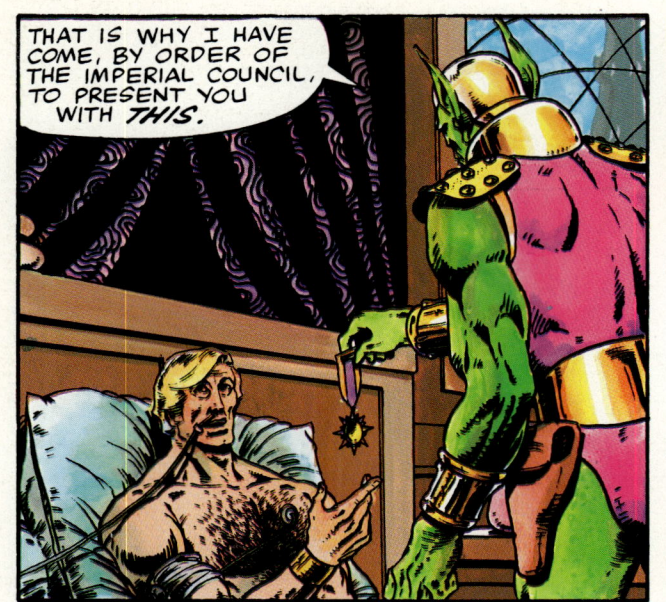

THAT IS WHY I HAVE COME, BY ORDER OF THE IMPERIAL COUNCIL, TO PRESENT YOU WITH *THIS.*

IT'S...THE ROYAL SKRULL MEDAL OF VALOR...

I *SALUTE YOU,* CAPTAIN!

MAY YOUR PASSING BE *SWIFT* AND YOUR AFTERLIFE REWARD *GREAT.*

HOW DO YOU LIKE THAT...

...THE *SKRULLS,* YOUR WORST ENEMIES, GIVE YOU A MEDAL. BUT WHAT DO YOUR OWN PEOPLE DO TO HONOR YOU?

ZIP! NOTHING! I'VE LOST TRACK OF HOW MANY TIMES YOU GOT THEIR FAT OUT OF THE FIRE!

BUT IN THE END I *TURNED* ON THE KREE EMPIRE, RICK.

I'M ON THE SUPREME INTELLIGENCE'S *BLACK-LIST.*

THEY DON'T GIVE MEDALS TO *TRAITORS.*

BUT IT ALL SEEMS SO UNFAIR.

I DON'T KNOW ABOUT THAT, RICK. I MAY BE IGNORED BY AN UN-GRATEFUL HOME-WORLD...

...BUT I'VE A *GOOD WOMAN*, WHO I LOVE, BY MY SIDE.

I'VE ALSO MANY FRIENDS, *FRIENDS* ANY MAN WOULD VALUE.

SO LET THE KREE KEEP THEIR SILLY *MEDALS* AND *HONORS*.

WHO NEEDS THEM?

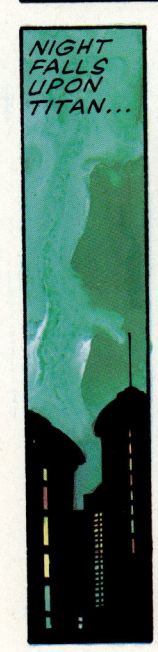

NIGHT FALLS UPON TITAN...

...AND FINDS THAT, FOR SOME, THE DAY'S WORK CON-TINUES.

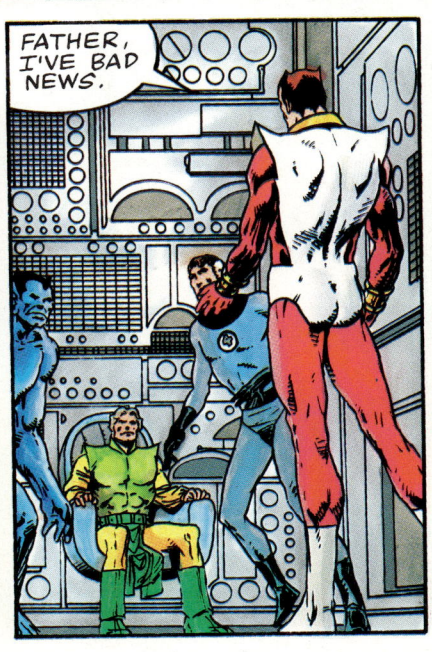

FATHER, I'VE BAD NEWS.

MAR-VELL HAS FALLEN INTO A *COMA.*

HE WAS THE *BEST* AMONG US. I WOULD HAVE GIVEN *ANYTHING* TO HAVE SAVED HIM.

IT'S ALL SO *UNFAIR*.

...SO UNFAIR.

SO UNFAIR SO UNFAIR SO UNFAIR SO UNFAIR

UNFAIR UNFAIR UNFAIR UNFAIR UNFAIR UNFAIR UNFAIR

...LIFE.

IN A SUB-BASEMENT TOMB. IN THE MIDST OF DEATH...

HE HEARS THE CALL AND MUST ANSWER.

ONE LAST TASK.

UP TOWARDS THE PALACE LEVELS HE CLIMBS, AND AS HE GOES, A STRANGE METAMORPHOSIS OCCURS.

DOWN FAMILIAR, WOOD PANELED HALLWAYS HE STALKS.

AT LAST HE STOPS.

THE SILENT ROYAL BED CHAMBER BECKONS LIKE THE DEATH HE LOVES.

HIS GOAL LIES WITHIN. NOTHING MUST STAND IN HIS WAY.

NOTHING.

WHO?

THANOS! HOW?! YOU'RE SUPPOSED TO BE...

...DEAD!

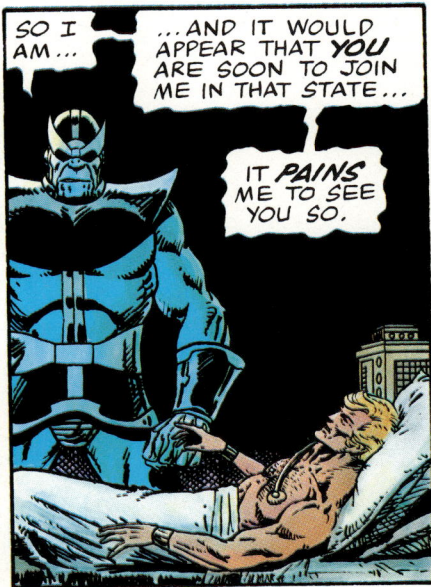

SO I AM...

...AND IT WOULD APPEAR THAT YOU ARE SOON TO JOIN ME IN THAT STATE...

IT PAINS ME TO SEE YOU SO.

FRAIL, ILL, DECAYED, SLOWLY WITHERING AWAY...

I'VE ALWAYS HAD GREAT RESPECT FOR YOU, MAR-VELL.

YOU HAVE ALWAYS BEEN MY GREATEST FOE, MY ARCH NEMESIS.

FOR ONE SUCH AS YOU, DEATH SHOULD NOT COME GNAWING LIKE SOME VERMIN.

FOR YOU, DEATH SHOULD BE...

...A GLORIOUS EVENT!

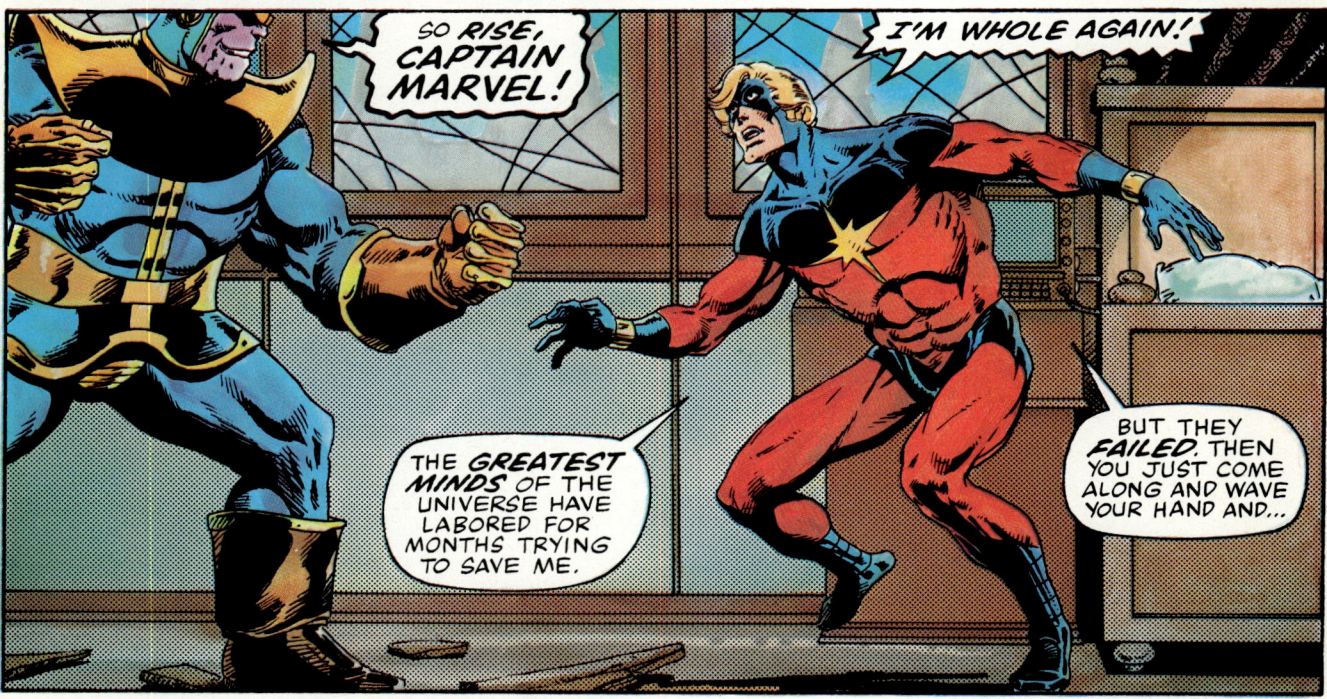

SO RISE, CAPTAIN MARVEL!

I'M WHOLE AGAIN!

THE GREATEST MINDS OF THE UNIVERSE HAVE LABORED FOR MONTHS TRYING TO SAVE ME.

BUT THEY FAILED. THEN YOU JUST COME ALONG AND WAVE YOUR HAND AND...

...I'M WELL AGAIN.

HOW?

WHY?

BECAUSE I AM THANOS, WHO IS DEATH AND THE LOVER OF DEATH.

I HAVE RETURNED FROM THE DARKNESS FOR ONE LAST, MAGNIFICENT BATTLE...

...WITH YOU.

FOR LIFE ITSELF IS NAUGHT BUT THE FIRST STEP TO *ETERNITY*, AND SETS ITS *TONE*.

YOUR TIME IS SPENT. YOUR FATE IS CAST.

SO IT *BEGINS*. SO IT *ENDS*.

LOOK NOW UPON YOUR PAST. BEAR WITNESS TO THE *HARVEST OF DEATH* YOU HAVE REAPED.

OLD FOES OF MINE WHO HAVE *DIED...*

...RETURNING FROM THE GRAVE!

RETURNING TO SHOW YOU THE WAY.

THANOS... HE SHATTERED LIKE A STATUE?!

FOR THAT IS ALL THAT IS LEFT OF ME IN THIS PLANE.

LIKE ALL MEN, I AM FINITE AND ACCEPT IT.

ILLUSION...

YOUR ARROGANCE IS NOBLE, BUT FUTILE; JUST, BUT USELESS.

IT IS THE WAY OF MAN, THE ONLY WAY WE KNOW HOW TO PLAY THE GAME.

ILLUSION...

BUT THE CONTEST IS OVER AND SHE COMES FOR YOU.

ARE YOU READY FOR HER?

AS READY AS I GUESS I'LL EVER BE.

SHE IS THE BRIDGE TO ETERNITY. HER CARESS IS PEACE.

DO NOT FEAR HER FOR SHE IS MERELY THAT WHICH AWAITS US ALL.

IT IS NOT THAT I FEAR HER,

IT'S JUST THAT...

...I NO LONGER NEED...

...THE ILLUSION.

SO IT ENDS...

TA-TUT TA-TUT TA-TUT TA-TUT TA........

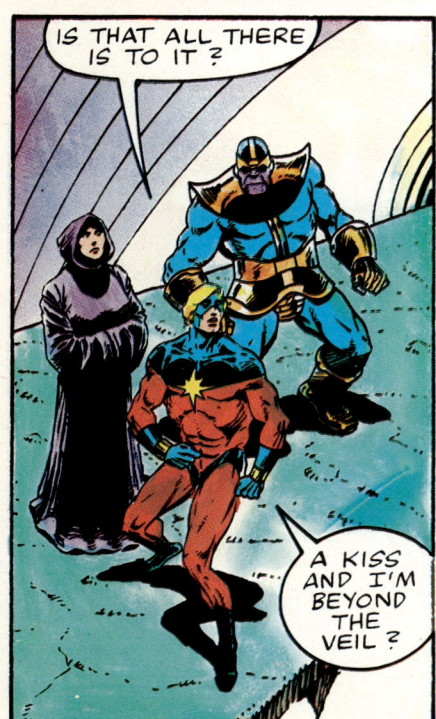

IS THAT ALL THERE IS TO IT?

A KISS AND I'M BEYOND THE VEIL?

I EXPECTED MORE.

THERE IS MORE, IT AWAITS US.

TAKE HER HAND.

SHE WILL LEAD US ON OUR JOURNEY.

SHE WILL SHOW US THAT THIS IS NOT THE END...